# TRIBADISM 3

---

## THE ART OF LESBIAN LOVE

## VICTORIA RUSH

# VOLUME 46

JADE'S EROTIC ADVENTURES - BOOK 46

# COPYRIGHT

*For the uninhibited...*

# WANT TO AMP UP YOUR SEX LIFE?

*Sign up for my newsletter to receive more free books and other steamy stuff. Discover a hundred different ways to wet your whistle!*

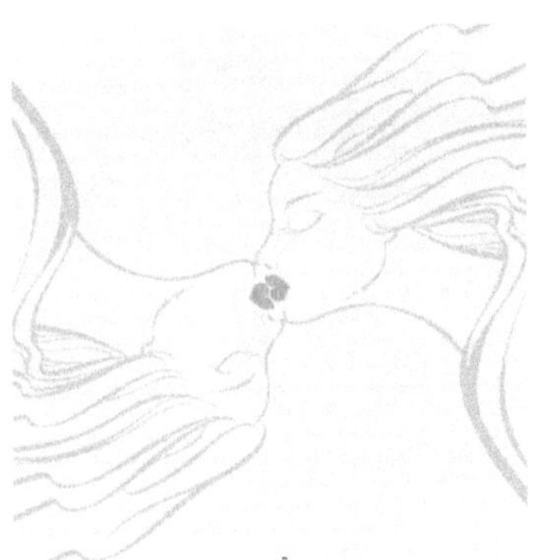

Victoria Rush Erotica

**1**

---

After the second day of our workshop ended, a few of the girls decided to go out for dinner together, where we speculated what Laila had planned for the final phase. She'd hinted about bringing some toys into the mix and we wondered who this new mystery guest would be that she'd promised would take our tribbing experience to the next level. But mostly, everybody just wanted to talk about how *hot* it was watching Laila, Mimi, and me grinding our bodies together in the pulsating shower spray of Laila's bathtub.

After teasing me about how I was the only one invited to participate in the last Waterfall exercise, Hailey and Trinity returned with me to my hotel room, where the three of us relived the experience while adding a few of our own new positions. By the following morning, everybody was pumped up and dripping in anticipation of the exciting conclusion to our hands-on workshop.

Laila greeted each of us warmly at the door to her West Side apartment, and as we nibbled on croissants and fresh fruit, I noticed something new – a small tube of lube had been placed beside each of our yoga mats. After everybody changed into fresh robes, we took our customary positions around the circle while Laila sat on the futon in the middle, placing a small duffel bag by her side.

"Good morning, ladies," she said. "Did you all have a restful and relaxing evening?"

"I'm not sure I'd call it *relaxing*, exactly," Hailey smiled, winking at me and Trinity. "But we sure rested pretty soundly by the time we finally got to sleep."

"Your bodies probably had some catching up to do after all the exercise we had yesterday," Laila chuckled. "I hope you've recharged your batteries, because today we're going to step up the action to a whole new level."

Piper squinted her eyes, shaking her head in disbelief.

"It's hard to imagine how many more ways we can connect our bodies together after all the positions we've already tried," she said.

"Maybe that's because up to now, we've been limited to connecting our bodies only *skin to skin*," Laila nodded, unzipping the top of her duffel bag. "Today, we're going to introduce some new tools to raise the excitement level even higher."

She reached into the bag and pulled out a long, double-sided, flexible dildo, waving it playfully in the air.

"Would you like to be our first volunteer of the day to help me demonstrate how this works, Piper?"

Piper smiled as she started to pull off her robe.

"I'm pretty sure I can guess how it works. I was wondering when you were finally going to ask me to join you on center stage."

By now, everybody had grown comfortable getting naked in front of one another, and as she crawled on all fours toward the middle of the circle, we all stared at her tight ass and dripping slit.

"It might look pretty obvious," Laila said, bending the silicone dildo in her hands after Piper joined her on the futon. "But because this dildo is flexible, there are almost infinite ways we can use it. In fact, you can pretty much use it for supplementary stimulation in *any* of the positions we've demonstrated so far. But for this first demonstration, I'd like us to try a modified version of the classic scissor position that I like to call *Tongue in Groove*."

"I like the sound of that," Piper smiled.

"Okay," Laila nodded. "To get started, I want you to lay down face-up on the futon with your knees slightly bent and legs parted..."

Piper assumed the position then Laila lay down in a similar position with her head at the other end, and their pussies separated by about six inches.

"You might want to use some lube I've placed beside each of your mats to make the initial insertion a little easier," Laila said, reaching for the bottle beside her.

"There's no need on my part," Piper said, rolling her hips excitedly. "I'm already plenty wet and slippery."

Laila raised her head and peered at Piper's glistening vulva, then she placed one end of the double-dildo against her opening, slowly pressing it inside her.

"Unghh," Piper groaned, shifting her hips forward. "That definitely feels different from anything we've tried so far."

"If you remember from my last workshop," Laila nodded. "The main body of the clitoris is actually on the *inside*, so this sex aid helps to stimulate the additional sensitive areas we can't reach with the other techniques. Including of course, the *G-Spot*, which is the secret spot for expressing your female ejaculation."

"Yes, I remember," Piper grunted. "I can already feel it stimulating me there."

"And the nice thing about this particular toy," Laila said, inserting the other end into her slit as she pushed her hips closer toward Piper. "Is that it can stimulate *both* of our G-Spots while we rock our bodies together."

As the two women began to roll their hips together in unison, the long instrument sunk deeper into their holes until their vulvas touched.

"Oh my God," Piper panted, moving her feet forward and placing them beside Laila's stomach while interlocking their legs. "This feels incredible tribbing your pussy with a dildo pressed inside me. But I'm finding it a bit difficult to get any friction against my clit..."

Laila titled her body forty-five degrees and pressed her knee between Piper's angled leg.

"The good thing about using this type of sex aid," she said. "Is that you can move your body into any position while still keeping it connected between the two of us. Try turning a little onto your side and pressing your leg against mine. That way, you'll be able to rub your clit against the inside of my thigh."

Piper followed her instructions and began moaning more deeply, and I smiled watching the two women, admiring Laila's skill at helping each of us expand our horizons while learning new sex positions. As she began rocking her hips more forcefully against Laila's pussy, I noticed many of the other girls moving their hands softly under their robes while they mimicked her movement.

As usual, Laila paused just before Piper was about to climax, and the pretty redhead sighed when the instructor separated their bodies. She pulled the dripping dildo out of

Piper's pussy and placed it on the futon beside her, then raised her head, peering around the circle.

"Are the rest of you guys ready to give this a try now?" she smiled.

"Damn straight," Hailey growled.

"Okay then," Laila nodded. "Everybody pair up with your nearest partner, then we'll shift positions with the next demonstration. You know the drill, Piper..."

As Piper frowned and sulked back toward the perimeter of the circle, I smiled, patting the mat next to me, inviting her to join me. Besides the fact that I was eager to help her finish getting off, I was throbbing at the thought of feeling her dripping pussy against mine.

Laila handed out fresh dildos to each pairing in the group, and after explaining that each toy had been properly sanitized, everyone quickly assumed the new Tongue in Groove position. I didn't waste any time placing the toy between Piper's and my legs, and it slid effortlessly into our slippery holes. As soon as our pussies touched, we both rolled over onto our sides, rubbing our thighs together.

"Holy shit," I groaned. "Laila wasn't kidding when she said this would elevate the experience to a whole new level."

"Just when you thought it couldn't get any better," Piper nodded, rocking her hips in unison with me.

I tilted my head down, trying to peer at her through our maze of twisted legs.

"Are you getting enough friction against your clit?"

"Yes," she panted, grabbing the sides of my ass and pulling me harder toward her. "It won't take long for me now. Are you getting close?"

"I'm moving there," I said, squeezing her leg more firmly. "Can you hold out a little longer? I'm enjoying this far too much to come so quickly. I want to feel you squirting on me when I come..."

"Okay," Piper grunted. "But with this dildo pushing up against my G-Spot, it's going to be difficult..."

I separated my legs a few inches to ease up on the friction of our inner thighs rubbing against our clits.

"Slow down and savor the feeling," I said. "Can you feel it moving inside you when I rock my hips?"

"Yes," she groaned. "Fuck me with your big dick, Jade. This feels even better with you *inside* me."

"Yes, baby," I purred, fucking her slowly while I grasped her flexing buttocks.

I could hear the sounds of the other women around the circle groaning along with us, and when I tilted my head to peer at the couple next to me, I saw Trinity's muscular ass flexing a few feet away while she and Ashley panted loudly. Then I glanced down to peer at Piper, and noticed her watching Becky and Paige on the opposite side as Paige's portly caboose slapped against her partner.

"I don't know how much longer I can hold out," Piper grunted, scrunching up her face. "This is too much of a turn-on watching all the other girls rubbing their hips together, knowing they've got a big dildo planted deep inside their pussies..."

"It's okay, babe," I said, feeling the pleasure rapidly building inside my pelvis. "I'm almost there too–"

"Jade–" Piper groaned, grabbing my ass and pulling me hard against her. "I can't hold it any longer. *Ngahhh!*"

When I felt her squirting against my pussy and shaking in the throes of a powerful orgasm, I also quickly lost control. The pressure of the dildo against my G-Spot only served to increase the force of my ejaculation, and as we squealed and held onto one another tightly, our combined juices squirted out between the sides of our thighs, spraying both of us in a warm, glorious shower. It didn't take long for the rest of the girls to also reach their crescendo, and we watched wide-eyed as one couple after another climaxed while scissoring their hips together with the big dildo deeply embedded inside their pussies.

*Talk about raising the stakes,* I smiled, peering over at Laila as she reached into her duffel bag for the next toy in her bag of tricks.

## 2

A fter everybody had a chance to recover and return to their positions in the circle, Laila peered at the group and smiled.

"So what did you all think?" she said. "Did you find the dildo enhanced the experience?"

"Hell, yes!" Trinity said. "Not to mention increasing the intensity of my squirting!"

"That's the idea," Laila nodded. "But to be fair, this dildo acts much like a man's penis, penetrating deep inside your vagina. If you remember from my last workshop, the G-spot is only a couple of finger joints inside your opening."

"Do you have a *different* toy to focus on that spot?" Trinity asked.

"Indeed I do," Laila smiled, reaching into her bag and pulling out a powder-blue, C-shaped object with two bulbous ends. "This toy is called the We-Vibe, and besides being perfectly curved to massage your G-Spot, it has the added luxury of a built-in *vibrator* to magnify the stimulation."

She reached into the case and pulled out another powder-blue-colored object and held it up for us to see.

"Plus, it comes with a separate remote control for adjusting the intensity of the vibrations."

"How does it work exactly?" Trinity said, squinting at the unusual shaped vibrator.

"Technically, it's meant for solo stimulation, but if you and your partner get in the right position, you can slip one end in *each* of your pussies to stimulate your G-Spots at the same time."

"Holy shit," Trinity said, squirming on her mat. "Can I be your first volunteer to give this one a try?"

"Absolutely," Laila chuckled, patting the futon beside her.

"How would you like me to position myself this time?" Trinity said, sitting down excitedly beside her.

"In this case," Laila said, "the optimal position is lying face-to-face with our knees pulled up toward our chest, resting our mounds on top of one another. I like to call this position *Snug as a Bug* because once the device is inserted, well I think you'll get the idea soon enough."

"Do you want me on the top or the bottom?" Trinity smiled.

"Why don't you go on the bottom so I can have a bit more control and show the rest of the group the best way to move our bodies?"

"You mean so you can decide when to *stop* just as I'm on the verge of coming!" Trinity chuckled.

"I just like to save the best part for you to share with your *own* partners," Laila smiled.

"I suppose that means you'll be in charge of the remote control too?" Trinity said, raising an eyebrow.

"This thing can be dangerous in the wrong hands," Laila

said, holding onto the remote tightly. "I'm not sure I can trust you to hand it back to me before we're finished."

"As long as *I'll* be the one controlling it when I continue with the other girls," Trinity nodded.

"That'll be between you and your partner," Laila smiled. "Now lie down and assume the position."

Trinity rolled over onto her back and lifted her knees to reveal her glistening vulva. Then Laila positioned herself overtop of her upturned thighs and lowered her pussy until their mounds touched.

"Do you need some lube before we get started?" she said, reaching behind her ass to position the We-Vibe in front of their openings.

"What do *you* think?" Trinity said, rolling her wet pussy against Laila's.

"Okay," Laila smiled, pressing the two ends of the object into their slits. "This requires a bit of careful maneuvering to insert it from behind, but once you slip the ends into your opening, it should slide in pretty easily..."

"*Fuck* yes," Trinity grunted, feeling the bulbous tip entering her hole. "This one's a bit of tighter fit. I see why you call this position Snug as a Bug."

"It has some reinforcement in the middle to hold it firmly against the walls of your pussy," Laila nodded.

"Mmm," Trinity nodded, rolling her hips sexily. "I can feel it pressing against my G-Spot. It's quite different from the last dildo we used."

Laila smiled as she lifted the remote control with her right hand, pressing one of the buttons.

"It gets even better when you activate the *vibrate* function."

"Oh my God," Trinity rasped, twisting her hips against Laila's. "That feels incredible."

"And the nice thing about this position is that we can also rub our clits together while we're receiving stimulation internally."

Trinity raised her head, peering between her legs at their joined pussies.

"Have you got *your* side turned on too?" she asked.

Laila tapped another button on the remote, and a second motor began softly buzzing.

"I do now," she grunted.

"Mmm," Trinity smiled, pulling her knees up higher to tilt her pussy into closer contact with Laila. "Why don't you let us go *all the way* this time? I won't have any trouble coming a second time this way."

Laila groaned while she tapped the Up arrow on the remote control to increase the intensity of the vibration on both ends.

"I might have to break my rule in this case," she said. "As long as you promise to save a little for your next partner."

"Maybe just a little," Trinity grinned, rocking her hips more forcefully against Laila's pussy.

As the two women slapped their hips together with the curved vibrator joining their pussies like a big staple, everybody around the circle looked on with their mouths agape.

"Holy fuck," Piper said, sitting next to me watching their vulvas grinding against one another. "That just might be the sexiest position I've seen so far."

"No kidding," I said, pushing two fingers deep into my throbbing pussy. "Talk about a view to a kill. I'd *die* to be in Trinity's position right now."

"Your turn will come soon enough," Piper smiled, placing her hand overtop of mine as I began fuck myself watching the two women.

"Oh God," Trinity panted from the center of the circle.

"Turn that thing up to the maximum setting. I'm going to come hard soon..."

Laila tapped the up arrows for both sides of the device, and within seconds both women were groaning loudly while they gyrated their hips wildly against one another, kissing each other passionately.

"That's it, baby," I hissed from the other side of the circle. "Come for momma. Let's see you *both* squirt this time."

Suddenly, Trinity screamed as she wrapped her legs around Laila's hips, squirting strong jets of fluid out of the sides of her pussy over Laila's raised ass. When she felt Trinity coming, Laila grunted loudly and within seconds, both women were squealing and spraying their partner's asses with powerful squirts from their convulsing pussies. Soon after, everyone else around the circle began groaning as their bodies convulsed with their fingers deeply embedded inside their pussies.

"Oh my God," Piper panted, pulling her wet hand out of her dripping pussy. "Something tells me this next exercise is going to be a little faster than the others."

After Laila and Trinity came down from their orgasms and Trinity returned to her mat, Laila instructed everyone to move over one position in the circle. With Piper eager to reconnect with her previous partner Paige, I quickly shifted over to pair up with Trinity.

"Fancy meeting *you* again," she smiled, noticing my wet right hand. "It looks like you're already warmed up."

"I couldn't help myself, watching you two rubbing your pussies together with that vibrator," I nodded. "Let's just say I won't be needing any lube for this one."

"Me neither," Trinity laughed, watching Laila passing out new We-Vibes to each of the couples around the circle. "Do you have a preference for which position you'd like to be in?"

"I think it's *your* turn to be on top this time," I smiled.

"Does that mean I also get to operate the remote control?" she grinned.

"Absolutely," I said, flopping onto my back and lifting my knees. "Just make sure you don't leave me hanging like Laila has a habit of doing."

"I wouldn't dream of it," Trinity said, crawling on top of me and pressing my thighs onto my chest as she lowered her ass over mine.

"Mmm," I purred, feeling her wet vulva pressing against mine. "I hardly even need the vibrator. You could make me cum just by rubbing your sweet pussy against mine."

"Maybe," she smiled, reaching behind her to insert the dildo. "But I have a feeling you're going to like it even more with a little extra help..."

"Ungh," I groaned when I felt the thick end of the curved dildo pressing inside me. "I think you might be right."

After both ends were pushed all the way inside our slits, Trinity didn't waste any time pressing the buttons on the remote to activate the internal vibrations.

"Holy fuck," I grunted, feeling the device throbbing against my G-Spot. "I've used this once or twice before, but never with another girl at the same time. This is *way* better than going solo."

"Yes," Trinity mewed, leaning her body down on top of mine and pressing our tits together. "This way, we get to stimulate a few *other* parts at the same time."

As we thrust our tongues into each other's mouths and began to roll our hips together, Trinity tapped the Up button on the remote, gradually ramping up the intensity of the pulsations.

"You're such a tease," I said, grinding my hips against hers.

"Two can play this game," she grinned. "Laila's not the *only* one who can keep you waiting."

"Maybe so," I smiled. "But there's still half a day left in the workshop. If we end up reconnecting again, I can just as easily turn the tables on you."

"Oh?" she said, lifting her face a few inches to peer at me with a raised eyebrow. "I'm not sure you're in a position to be making idle threats right now. I've already *had* my jollies, remember?"

"But you said you'd have no difficulty coming a second time with your new part–"

Suddenly, Trinity flipped the switch to the maximum intensity, lowering her face onto mine.

"Unngh," I grunted into her mouth, feeling my orgasm approaching like a freight train.

"Fuck, babe," I hissed. "I'm gonna cum so hard..."

"Yes, Jade," Trinity growled. "Spray your juices all over me. *Nobody* can squirt like you."

"You better get ready," I panted, feeling the floodgates beginning to open. "Cause I'm gonna cum like a fire hose. Here it comes, baby..."

Suddenly, I felt my insides clamping tightly against the bulbous tip of the curved dildo, forcing the ejection of my juices onto the outsides of Trinity's thighs between the dildo firmly embedded in our holes.

"Yes, Jade," Trinity gasped, reaching her second powerful climax of the morning. "Fuck, *this* one is even stronger than my last one. *Ngahh!*"

As we held onto each other tightly, listening to the

sounds of the other women around the circle groaning in simultaneous pleasure, we both smiled, kissing each other passionately.

"I hope I get another turn with you before we're done today," she smiled, rolling her breasts over mine. "Something tells me we're not done finding new ways to incorporate a dick into our tribbing experience."

**3**

———

It took a little longer for everyone to come down from their powerful orgasms using the We-Vibe, and after we cleaned up our dripping mats, we paused for a half-hour buffet lunch. While we nibbled on warm hot dogs, we chuckled at Laila's cheeky homage to the dildos we'd added to our latest tribbing exercises. None of us knew what to expect next, and as I peered among the group resting comfortably around the circle, I wondered who I'd be paired up with next.

After we finished eating, Laila returned to her position in center of the room, unzipping her toy bag to take inventory of the remaining items inside.

"Looks like we're not done using the dildos yet," Trinity smiled, sitting next to me on the mat.

"It's too bad," I snickered. "After enjoying those juicy wieners, I could really go for a *real* cock right about now."

"Well, Laila did say we'd have another *guest* today," Trinity grinned. "Maybe your wish will still come true."

"Did everybody have a chance to stuff their bellies and

replenish their fluids?" Laila said, peering at everyone sitting eagerly in anticipation of the next event on the program.

"It wasn't just our *bellies* that we stuffed," Hailey grinned.

"And I'm not sure I replenished all of the *fluids* I lost after that last exercise," Ashley nodded.

"Yup," Laila chuckled. "That little We-Vibe really packs a punch."

"Speaking of punching," Paige interjected. "All of the dildos we've used so far have been kind of passive in the sense of staying in place once inserted. Sometimes it's kind of nice just to get a good *pounding*, if you know what I mean."

"I think I do," Laila smiled, reaching into the bag resting on the floor beside her. "And funnily enough, I brought an extra toy along with me today that might fit the bill."

She lifted a harness with a big, realistic-looking cock attached to the front and waved it playfully in the air.

"For those of you who like penetrative sex or playing the domme, I have just the thing. A strap-on dildo that gives you maximum control of the movement and pumping action of the faux penis."

"Fake or not," Paige said, staring at the big phallus with wide eyes. "That's a mighty big cock. Are you sure that thing will even fit inside us?"

"I dunno," Laila grinned. "Do you want to be the first to find out?"

"I thought you'd never ask," Paige said, while the rest of the girls chuckled.

As she crawled on all-fours toward the futon, we all stared at her magnificent, rotund, Rubenesque-sized ass. If there was going to be any *pounding* going on in this next exercise, Laila had picked the perfect candidate to demonstrate its use.

"Would you like me to give or receive?" Paige said, waving her butt next to the instructor.

Laila peered at her plump derriere and smiled.

"You know how I prefer to be the one in charge so I show the rest of the girls how it's done..." she said with a raised eyebrow.

"Yes," Paige huffed. "And also being the one to stop when it starts to get interesting."

"Well I might have to break my rule again with this next demonstration," Laila said, wrapping the harness straps around her waist and under her thighs. "Because this toy doesn't stimulate the external clitoris directly, I'm going to allow everyone to stimulate themselves *manually* while their partner is humping them from behind."

"Does that mean I can actually *come* this time if I want?" Paige said, widening her eyes.

"If you can keep up with me, yes," Laila smiled, shuffling around behind Paige's ass and pouring a drop of lube on the end of the phallus. "In fact, it's a good way to warm up before we get started."

"Oh, I'm plenty warmed up already," Paige said, swiping her butt against the side of the tool, making it swing from side to side.

"Okay," Laila nodded. "You can use this device in pretty much any of the previous positions we've practiced, but in this case, I'm going to use it in the doggy position, because well..."

She peered down and slapped Paige's ass softly.

"This bitch has got the perfect rump for humping from behind."

"Woof, woof!" Paige yelped playfully.

Laila grasped the end of the phallus with two fingers

then pointed it toward Paige's slit, slowly inserting it into her hole.

"*Still* think it's too big?" she grinned, pausing halfway.

"Are you kidding me?" Paige grunted, pushing her hips backwards toward Laila's hips. "I want *all* of it inside me. Fuck me with your big dick. I've been waiting for this for *three* days now."

Laila grabbed the sides of Paige's ass and sunk the dildo deep into her pussy, then she began rocking her hips forward and back, slapping the harness against her wet skin.

"Fuck yes," Paige growled. "Pound me with your big cock. *That's* what I'm talking about."

As Laila dug her fingers into the sides of Paige's ass and began to fuck her harder, the rest of us watched with wide eyes while we squirmed on our mats.

"Holy shit," Trinity said, watching Laila's ass cheeks flexing while she humped Paige's ass. "I usually like to be the domme in my relationships, but even *I'd* be happy to be on the receiving end of that sexy-ass dick."

"Come on," I said, sliding my fingers over her wet pussy. "Don't tell me you wouldn't like a piece of that exquisite ass?"

"If you twisted my arm, maybe," she grinned.

By now, Paige had lowered her *own* hand between her legs, trilling her clit while Laila fucked her from behind.

"That feels incredible," she panted, tilting her upper body down onto the futon to rest her shoulders while she jilled herself. "You better watch out when I come. Because I'm going to spray all over your stomach and pretty tits anytime now."

"Go for it, girl," Laila grunted, digging her nails into Paige's hips as she rocked her hips faster against her butt.

"Oh my God," Paige hissed. "Here it comes. Oh *fuckkkk!*"

Suddenly a huge spray jetted up out of Paige's hole, squirting in every direction as many of the women blinked when the spray reached them.

"Holy shit!" Trinity gasped, wiping a streak off the side of her cheek. "Okay, I lied. I *definitely* want to be the one doing the fucking with that chick."

"I thought so," I chuckled, watching Paige's ass cheeks trembling while her body shook in the throes of an intense orgasm.

It took Paige almost two minutes to come down from her high, and when Laila pulled out of her and sat beside her with the dripping dildo pointing up between her legs, Paige stroked it playfully with her hand.

"Thank you for letting me come," she said, kissing Laila on her cheek.

"It was my pleasure," Laila grinned.

"Actually," Paige said, leaning over to inspect the configuration of the harness more carefully. "This contraption doesn't actually stimulate *you* at the same time, does it?"

"That depends," Laila said, reaching into her bag and pulling out a small, bullet-shaped object. "There's a pouch under the base of the dildo where you can insert a small vibrator to enhance the stimulation for both of us if so desired."

"*Now* you tell me," Paige huffed. "Why didn't you insert it before?"

"I just wanted to give you a good-old-fashioned *fucking*," Laila smiled. "Without the aid of any extra stimulation."

"Well, it worked," Paige nodded. "Although I couldn't

help providing a little extra stimulation of my *own* while you were pounding my ass."

"And it's a such a pretty ass," Laila said, slapping the side of her cheek. "Now get over there and share that beautiful booty with some of the other girls. The rest of you know the routine by now..."

Trinity turned her head to peer at me and smiled.

"Do you mind–?"

"You go, girl," I grinned, reading her thoughts. "I wouldn't dare get between you and that fuckable ass when you're this worked up. Maybe later we'll have another chance to hook up..."

"Don't stray too far," she said, slipping over to Paige's mat while I moved in the opposite direction.

When everybody finished shifting positions, I ended up paired with the pretty young co-ed Becky this time.

"Hello again," I smiled, remembering the last time when we'd joined together in the reverse cowgirl position.

"Hey," she said. "That was one crazy ass demonstration, wasn't it?"

"Crazy ass is the perfect description," I nodded. "Maybe that's what Laila should name this one.

"Or maybe Booty Call," Becky said.

"I dunno," I grinned, holding out my hand as Laila passed us a new harness. "*Strap-on* has a nice ring to it."

"Totally," Becky chuckled. "Do you want to be the strap-*ee* or the strap-*er*?"

"Well, speaking of perfect asses," I said, peering down at her tight, young derriere. "If you're giving me a *choice*, the top position suits me just fine."

"Works for me. Did you want to try it with or without the vibrating bullet?"

"Doesn't hurt to give it a try," I smiled, slipping the plug into the pouch below the dildo and pressing the on-button.

"I like the sound of that," Becky said, listening to the purring motor and turning over to place herself on all fours.

"Do you mind if we try a different position?" I said.

"I don't see why not. Laila said we could use in pretty much any position. Which one did you have in mind?"

"I'd kind of like to *see* you while I'm fucking you," I smiled. "Why don't you lay down facing up so we can rub some other parts of our bodies together at the same time?"

"In the missionary position, you mean?"

"To start with," I laughed. "But we can adapt as we go, maybe switch it up halfway through."

"Definitely," Becky said, lying down on the mat and raising her knees to expose her pink vulva.

I looked at her glistening pussy and knelt down in front of her, pointing the tip of the dildo toward her hole.

"Do you need me to add lube?"

"I'm already plenty lubed up," she said, tilting her head down to watch tiny rivulets of juices seeping down over her ass.

"Mmm," I purred, pressing the rigid cock slowly inside her while pulling my thighs forward to squeeze her ass.

"Fuck, yes," Becky panted. "That definitely feels different from the other dildos we tried."

"There's nothing like having it connected to a real person on the other end," I nodded, pushing it all the way inside her. "Am I hurting you?"

"Only in all the right ways," Becky smiled.

I leaned forward to rest my body against hers, and as our tits meshed, I kissed her softly, thrusting my tongue inside her mouth. The feeling of being connected at the hips while echoing the sensation with our tongues took the experience to a whole new level. As we moaned in each other's mouths,

I pressed my mound down harder onto hers, feeling the vibration of the bullet below the dildo stimulating my clit. Becky lifted her knees and wrapped her legs around my waist, but I could tell from the movement of her hips that something was off.

"Is this working for you?" I said, lifting my head a few inches.

"I love the feeling of you fucking me from on top," she said. "But the angle of your cock is missing my sweet spot. I can feel the vibration from the bullet, but it's pulsing closer to my butthole than my clit."

"Yeah, I was wondering about that," I nodded. "As much fun as it is to feel your body rubbing up against me while I'm making love to you, if we're going to take maximum advantage of this setup, I'm going to have to do this to you from behind."

Becky paused when I pulled my dripping tool out of her hole.

"I can think of *another* way we can position our bodies to place the vibrator in the right position," she smiled.

She flipped over onto her stomach and tilted her ass upwards, peering at me over her shoulder.

"Lie on top of me," she said. "I want to feel your tits rubbing on my back while you fuck me."

"If you insist," I smiled, positioning the tip of the dildo between her cheeks and slowly lowering myself overtop of her while I pressed it inside her pussy.

"Better?" I said.

"Better," she purred, squeezing her buttock muscles against my stomach as I began to hump her from behind.

I could feel the pouch containing the bullet pressing between her thighs, and I tilted my hips down a little further to rest it against her clit above my thrusting phallus.

"*Much* better," she groaned, grabbing the sides of our yoga mat with clenched hands.

"Me too," I panted, beginning to fuck her harder while I interlaced my fingers with hers.

"*Fuck* me, Jade," Becky hissed as our mat began sliding forward and back on the hardwood floor. "Fuck me hard. I want to feel you sinking your dick all the way inside me when I come."

"Fuck yes," I grunted, pretending I was a man fucking her from behind.

It had been a long time since I'd been fucked by anybody this way, and I reveled in the raw sexuality of the act while jerking my body hard above her.

"Yes, baby," Becky moaned, squeezing my fingers harder. "Don't stop. I'm going to come all over your big cock any second now..."

"Let it go, hun," I said, feeling the pulsations of the vibrator pressing harder against my clit as I pushed my hips firmer against her cheeks.

"Oh God..." Becky shuddered, teetering on the edge of climax.

Suddenly she groaned like a wild animal and pressed her mound hard onto the yoga mat as her whole body began shaking like she was having an epileptic fit. When I felt her coming, I soon also lost control, and for the next minute both of us held onto each other tightly while we howled in euphoric ecstasy.

When we finally finished coming, I peered around the circle watching the other women paired up in various positions, humping their partners while they groaned in delight. Then I glanced over at Trinity's mat and our eyes met just as she plunged her big dick deep into Paige's butt, jerking her body in the midst of her own rapturous orgasm.

**4**

———

After everyone finished coming from their latest pairing, they slowly decoupled and returned to their normal positions awaiting the next exercise. I thought it was funny that many of the girls didn't even bother to remove their harnesses, and as we sat cross-legged on our mats with our pink dildos poking up between our legs, Laila nodded at us and smiled.

"I noticed that many of you chose to try new positions while using that little sex toy," she said.

"Yeah, except it wasn't so *little*," Becky grinned.

"Did you enjoy the sensation of having someone actively moving the dildo inside you this time?"

"Yes," Becky said. "It almost felt like an actual man fucking me for a moment."

"It's too bad you limited this workshop only to *women*," Hailey nodded. "There's nothing like the feeling of a real dick to replace the sensation of an artificial penis."

"It's funny you mention that," Laila said, reaching into her bag to lift a small bell, tinkling it softly in her hand.

A few moments later, a tall naked man emerged from

the rear hallway, walking seductively toward the center of the room. We gasped when we saw his buff physique and handsome face, unable to take our eyes off his large, swinging prick between his legs.

"This is Alessandro," Laila smiled, kissing him softly on his lips when he sat down beside her on the futon. "He's graciously agreed to join us for the last portion of our workshop to add a little extra spice to our tribbing exercises."

"How will that *work* exactly?" Ashley said, shaking her head. "I mean, as impressive as he is, he's only got one cock to compete with two pussies."

"So it would seem," Laila nodded. "But as was the case when we added an extra *woman* into the mix yesterday, you might be surprised at all the different ways the three of you can join together."

"Just in the *middle*, you mean?" Paige said, pinching her eyebrows. "Or are you including the use of hands and mouths and other body parts?"

"Well, we did name this workshop Tribadism for a reason," Laila smiled. "I thought to keep it interesting, that we'd keep it a hands-free experience."

"You also said it was going to be an *all-girls* workshop," Trinity said, slightly miffed that Laila had broken her promise to make it a lesbian-only experience.

"That's true," Laila nodded. "And to permit those of you who prefer only to have sex with women, I've unlocked my bedroom for your personal use. Anybody who doesn't want to participate in this final segment is welcome to retire to my private chambers to continue your exercises. Of course, you're also welcome to stay here and just *watch* if you prefer."

There was a long pause in the room while everybody peered at one another, then they returned their gaze to the center of the room, staring at the hunky adonis sitting next to Laila.

"Okay then," Laila smiled. "Who'd like to be the first to help demonstrate our first three-way combination I like to call the *Bottle Rocket*?"

Hailey and Ashley were the first to eagerly raise their hands, and as they crawled toward the center of the ring with their tits swaying on their chests, I noticed Alessandro's dick slowly beginning to rise between his legs. By the time they joined him sitting on opposite sides of Laila, his erection was pointing straight up, rising all the way up to the bottom of his six-pack abs.

"Now I see why you call it a *bottle*," Hailey grinned, peering at Alessandro's magnificent organ. "That thing is even bigger than the strap-on dildo we were using."

"Plus, it's warm and edible, just like the hot dogs you enjoyed over lunch," Laila grinned. "Not to mention having a few *extra* dynamic features the plastic dildo doesn't have–"

"Thus the *rocket* part of the position description," Ashley nodded, noticing the pre-cum dripping out of the tip of Alessandro's tool.

"True," Laila nodded. "Although I'm going to ask Alessandro to hold off the best for last. We've still got two more boy-on-girl-on-girl positions to practice before we finish up our workshop, and I'll want him to stay hard and erect so everyone who wants a piece of him can also have their turn."

"Not if *we* have anything to say about it," Hailey said, tracing the tip of her index finger along the underside of his shaft, causing his dick to twitch and flap against his belly.

"We'll see if he can resist your charms," Laila smiled. "But remember, no hands allowed. This is strictly going to be a *pussy-on-pussy* demonstration."

"How exactly will we do that with only one dick?"

"Alessandro?" Laila said, nodding toward the Italian stud.

When he lay down on the futon face-up with his hard-on rising ten inches above his belly, all the women around the circle gasped. I noticed many of them already had their hands between their legs playing with their pussies, and I smiled at how fluid their sexual proclivities were when the opportunity presented.

"Alright," Laila smiled, watching Alessandro's dick flapping excitedly against his belly. "For this first exercise, I want each of you girls to sit facing one another with Alessandro's cock positioned between your pussies. You may find it easier to wrap your legs around each other's asses for extra stability."

Ashley and Hailey peered at one another for a moment, then Ashley crawled atop Alessandro's stomach, sliding her crotch up against the front of his pole. Soon after, Hailey copied her movement, positioning herself in the other direction while she lowered her ass over his balls. When the two women joined their hips together, they wrapped their arms around each other's backs, pressing their breasts together.

"Mmm," Ashley groaned, rocking her hips against Hailey while she ground her wet pussy against Alessandro's hard pole. "This feels a lot better than a silicone dick."

"And *harder*," Hailey nodded, pulling herself closer to her partner.

"What about you, Alessandro?" Laila said, watching the trio grinding their hips together. "How's it working for you?"

"It's *working*," he grunted with a sly smile, caressing the sides of Ashley's flexing buttocks.

While everybody in the circle chuckled nervously, the threesome began rocking their hips in tandem. From my position at the side of the group, I could see Alessandro's brown pole thrusting up between the two women's bare mounds with their skin glistening in the soft light streaming in from the living room window. I wasn't sure if the wetness was coming from the precum dribbling out of the top of his prick or from the lubrication rapidly building up between the two women's legs. Either way, it was obvious that all three of them were enjoying this new tribbing experience, if not the neighbors peering on with their spyglasses.

"Oh my God," Ashley panted, thrusting her tongue into Hailey's mouth while the two women wrapped their legs around each other's asses, pulling their pussies harder against Alessandro's flexing pole. "This is way better with a third person in the mix."

"Yeah," Hailey smiled. "Especially when it's a man."

"Are you going to be able to hold off there, big boy?" Laila said, watching Alessandro's face reddening as he tried to resist the urge to come while the two women massaged his dick with their wet pussies.

"I'm trying," he huffed, digging his fingers in deeper into the sides of Ashley's ass.

"You two better finish up there before Alessandro loses control," Laila smiled, peering over at Ashley and Hailey.

"You mean you're going to let us *come* this time?" Hailey said.

"It's not like we're going to be able to share him with all the other women around the circle," Laila nodded. "We've only got one flesh-and-blood cock to work with for the rest of the afternoon, so you better make the best of it while you have the chance."

"I'm getting close," Ashley panted, pressing her tits tighter against Hailey's chest. "How about you, Hailey?"

"I was kind of hoping to feel this big stud coming all over

my stomach when I let it rip," Hailey smiled. "But if that's going to be against the rules, maybe we can give him a little something to remember us by."

"I think I get your drift," Ashley nodded, pulling Hailey's face toward her while the two women kissed passionately.

As they began rocking their hips harder against Alessandro's flapping pole, Ashley grunted loudly, slapping her thighs hard against the side of Hailey's ass. Soon after, Hailey's buttock muscles started quivering as she locked her legs around Ashley's hips. Within seconds, both women were convulsing over Alessandro's turgid pole and he grimaced trying to resist the temptation to come, feeling Hailey spraying her juices over his tightening balls.

It didn't take long for most of the other women around the circle to begin coming also, and as I jilled myself watching the others climaxing, I peered over at Trinity, who had three fingers deeply embedded inside her pussy, shaking uncontrollably. I wasn't sure if she was getting more turned on watching the two women rubbing their pussies together or watching the sexy hunk pile driving his dick between the two of them, but either way, something told me she wasn't done participating in the tribbing exercises today.

## 5

-------

After Ashley and Hailey finished coming atop Alessandro's stomach, they rolled over onto the futon with giant grins on their faces.

"So do you still think one cock isn't enough for two pussies?" Laila smiled at the two girls.

"With a cock like that," Ashley grinned, peering at Alessandro's still rigid pole. "He could probably satisfy *three* pussies simultaneously."

"Are you sure we can't have a little more of him?" Hailey said, swiping her finger up his dripping erection. "It's a shame we couldn't have him *inside* of our pussies."

"It's only fair to share the spoils," Laila said, turning to peer at the rest of the women waiting patiently around the circle. "That is, assuming some of the *other* girls are interesting in taking a turn with him too?"

Piper and Paige didn't waste any time throwing up their hands, and as Hailey and Ashley reluctantly returned to their places in the group, the two new girls took their position beside Alessandro.

Laila excused herself for a moment, and when she

returned, she placed a strange triangle-shaped pillow in front of the threesome with a sly grin on her face.

"In this next exercise I call the *Downward Dog*, we're going to introduce a different kind of sex aid into the equation. This special pillow will allow you to raise your juicy parts into a position that will facilitate a more direct connection between your bodies."

"And by *direct*," Paige said, staring at Alessandro's flaring dick. "Do you mean we'll actually be allowed to *fuck* him this time?"

"Well, technically," Laila smiled. "I suppose *he'll* be doing the fucking, but yes."

"But only with one of us, right?" Piper said, pinching her eyebrows.

"Yes, although the second partner will have an opportunity to avail herself of certain of his other manly features."

"How so?" Piper said, shaking her head.

"First, we'll need to decide which of you wants to be on the bottom and which one will be on top."

"Given my more generous proportions," Paige chuckled. "I suppose I should be the one on the bottom of this particular stack."

"Okay then," Laila nodded. "I want you to lie down face-up and elevate your hips in the air by angling your back against one side of the pillow."

She moved the pillow behind Paige's ass, then she pushed it gently under her back until her legs and hips were propped two feet above the surface of the futon.

"How do I fit into this arrangement?" Piper said, glancing at Paige's exposed pussy as she waved her legs playfully in the air.

"This one's a bit of a convoluted formation, kind of like the game of Jenga," Laila smiled. "We have to insert the pieces in a particular order to keep it from falling over. And the next piece in the puzzle is going to be Alessandro."

She peered at Alessandro who'd already raised himself into a kneeling position on the other side of the pillow.

"Do you want to show the ladies how we're going to hold the pieces together?"

Alessandro smiled, then he turned around lying face down on the other side of the pillow, lifting his erection above Paige's open slit resting next to his hips at the top of the pillow.

"Would you like me to add some lube to make this easier?" he said, turning his head to look at Paige, whose shoulders were resting along with his at the base of the pillow.

"It shouldn't be necessary," Paige grinned, peering up at her dripping pussy. "It looks like I'm already producing plenty of my own lubrication."

"It appears that she's ready for you to insert your block into her hole," Laila smiled, continuing the Jenga imagery.

Alessandro raised his eyebrows, nodding toward Paige to confirm her assent, and she eagerly nodded back. As he lowered his hips toward her ass, his rod slowly sunk into her dripping slit. By the time he pressed it all the way inside, they looked like two cards teetering against one another at forty-five-degree angles.

"Unhhh," Paige groaned, feeling Alessandro filling her cavity.

"I'm beginning to understand your comparison of this position to the game of Jenga," Piper nodded, gazing at the two partners pinned together in an inverted position. "How exactly do *I* fit into the picture?"

"Well, there's actually a *couple* of ways you can position yourself," Laila said. "You can either lie on top of Paige in a reclined version of the missionary position or you can straddle her hips while standing up to give you a bit more control of the action."

"Not to mention a better *view*," Piper smiled, peering at Alessandro's tight balls nestled against Paige's slit while they rolled their hips seductively together.

"Yes," Laila nodded. "There's that advantage too."

Piper peered down at Paige, who was pulling her knees further down toward her chest, and grinned.

"Are you going to be okay if I take the superior position this time?" she asked.

"Way ahead of you, girl," Paige said, rocking her hips as Alessandro's tool began to move in and out of her pussy. "You're not the *only* one who'll be able to watch the action from this perspective."

Piper nodded and positioned her feet on opposite sides of Paige's hips facing Alessandro's upturned ass, then she slowly lowered her hips until her pussy pressed against Paige's mound and Alessandro's scrotum.

"Mmm," Paige moaned, watching Piper's juices rolling down the back of her overturned thighs. "Now *that's* picture you don't see every day."

"Oh my God," Piper shuddered, feeling Alessandro's tight balls sliding against her clit. "I had no idea when you said this was going to be a *tribbing* workshop that we'd be rubbing our bodies against so many interesting parts."

"How about you, Alessandro?" Laila said, smiling at Alessandro groaning while he plowed his dick in and out of Paige's warm pussy. "Is this something you ever imagined doing with two women?"

"Never like this," he grunted. "But it sure as hell won't be the *last* time."

While the rest of the girls looking on from the circle

chuckled, Becky and I shook our heads in amazement as we played with each other's pussies.

"Can you believe this?" she panted while I circled my fingers over her hardening clit.

"It's a pretty novel arrangement, to be sure," I nodded. "You gotta hand it to Laila to come up with such inventive positions to keep it interesting."

"*Interesting* is hardly the word for it," Becky grunted. "I'd give my left pinky to be on the receiving end of that dagger right now."

"Are you kidding me?" I said, pulling her hand harder against my throbbing cunt. "I'd give my left *tit* to have ten minutes alone with him."

Laila smiled watching the women around the circle looking on in rapt attention while they played with their pussies.

"The nice thing about this position," she continued, offering color commentary from the side. "Is that all *three* of the participants can rub their erogenous parts against one another at the same time."

"Mmm," Piper nodded, staring between her legs while she squatted over Alessandro's ball sac, sliding her clit over his bulge. "I can feel Paige's wet slit rubbing against mine while I hump Alessandro's balls."

"No shit," Paige huffed, staring up at Piper's backside while the pretty redhead rocked her ass over her splayed legs. "And I get to watch Piper's beautiful ass while she tribs my clit with her sweet pussy."

"What about you, Alessandro?" Laila smiled, turning her head to glance at the Italian stud. "Are you enjoying this two-way action too?"

"To put it mildly," he grunted, curling his fingers into the futon as Piper rubbed her pussy against his balls. "Maybe you should consider renaming this position *The Full Monty*. Because I've never been stimulated quite so perfectly in two places at the same time."

Laila chuckled, returning her attention to the two groaning women.

"I'm not sure how much longer he can hold out with you two stimulating his balls and his penis simultaneously. I think you girls better finish up soon before he loses his edge for our final demonstration."

"Fine with me," Paige grunted, pulling her knees harder down toward her chest. "I've been dying to watch Piper shower my tits ever since we started this crazy maneuver."

"It's not just your *tits* I'll be showering," Piper smiled as a flush began to spread over her freckled chest. "Get ready because this is going to be a big one..."

Moments later, she grunted loudly as her flexing thighs began to quake and she sprayed a fountain of juices down Paige's belly and over her shaking breasts.

"Holy shit," Paige growled, throwing her hands to her side and digging her nails into the futon as she came simultaneously.

When Alessandro felt Piper squirting over his balls and Paige's pussy clamping down over his throbbing dick, he squeezed his eyelids shut tightly and scrunched his face into a tortured grimace, summoning all of his strength to resist emptying his pent-up load deep into Paige's hole. It took almost a full minute for the two women to stop grunting and shaking, and by the time they finished, he was gasping like he'd completed a marathon.

"Now that was a beautiful sight to behold," Laila said, nodding at the threesome as they panted on top of one another. "Were you able to hold it together in the midst of that coordinated attack, Alessandro?"

"*Barely*," he panted. "I don't think I've ever had a more challenging task my entire life."

"That was quite an impressive performance," Laila nodded, turning to glance at the rest of the women still peering on with their mouths agape. "What do you say, ladies? Do you think our trio deserves a round of applause?"

It didn't take long for a loud cheer to encircle the room as everybody nodded in appreciation, wondering which of them would have the final chance to connect with the Italian adonis.

# 6

After the last exciting three-way hookup with Alessandro, we all took a short bio break, chatting amongst ourselves about what we thought Laila had cooked up for the grand finale. I thought it was a bit funny how virtually all of the women who'd signed up for the all-girls sex seminar had no reservations about mixing it up with the hung stud. I wasn't sure how Laila was going to choose between the large group of remaining women for who'd participate in the final turn, but the rivers of juices running down the inside of thighs betrayed my impatience at finding out.

After everyone finished freshening up, we returned to our positions in the circle, sitting buck naked and cross-legged on our yoga mats, eagerly anticipating the last exercise.

"So, what do you think, ladies?" Laila said with a smile. "Do you still think there's a limited number of ways women can trib their bodies together?"

"Not when you add a third person into the mix," Ashley smiled.

"Especially when it's a man," Paige grinned.

"Yes," Laila nodded, caressing Alessandro's trimmed pubis with the tips of her fingers. "There's an almost infinite number of ways we can create an exciting connection between two or three people. That's the beauty of having so many interesting parts to work with."

Becky shifted distractedly on her mat, staring at Alessandro's thickening tool as he peered out at the group of women waiting to have a turn with him.

"How were you planning on sharing that *particular* part with the rest of us?" she said. "Short of putting us on a rotating spit while he takes turns prodding us with his tenderizer, I don't see how this is going to work."

"That's not a bad idea," Laila laughed. "But since this is still a tribbing workshop, I'd like to give our last two partici-pants a chance to rub their bodies together while also giving Alessandro a chance to get in on the action."

"But there's eight of us left and only two spots remain-ing," Becky said. "How will you decide who gets the last poke at the pot?"

"I think the only fair way to do it," Laila said, reaching into the tote bag resting at her side. "Is to have a kind of lottery. But to make it more interesting, we're going to use a *different* kind of spinning ball to pick the winners."

She pulled out a handful of multi-colored small nerf balls and tossed them gently around the circle until everyone held one in their hands. Then she turned to Alessandro, whose prick had risen to full flagstaff and smiled.

"Are you up for this last exercise?" she said.

"Oh, I'm *up* for it alright," he grinned, spreading his legs apart.

"Okay," Laila said, peering back at the women squeezing

their balls excitedly in their hands. "The way we're going to do this is by having each of you toss your ball in the direction of Alessandro's penis. The two that end up closest to his dick will join him for our last exercise of the day. We'll start with Becky, then go clockwise around the circle."

Becky paused to focus on Alessandro's erection, placing the tip of her tongue on her upper lip as she concentrated. Then she threw her ball underhanded in the direction of his separated legs and it bounced over one of his thighs, resting a few inches behind his ass. She frowned, unhappy with her performance, then peered at the next woman sitting to her left.

As each of the women tossed their nerf balls toward Alessandro's flapping erection, a collection of balls collected around his hips, nestling up near the base of his testicles. When my turn came, I raised up on my knees, taking three practice swings, then I tossed my ball high in the air, bouncing it onto the surface of the futon. It bobbed a couple of times then hit his stomach, sliding down to wedge between his upturned dick and his abdomen.

"Woo hoo!" the rest of the girls shouted in admiration of my pitching skills.

Then all eyes turned toward Trinity, who held the last ball.

She copied my stance and leaned forward as far as she could, then she tossed her ball firmly with a hard swing of her arm. The ball landed on the edge of the futon and rolled toward Alessandro's balls, then it bounced up on top of the other balls, resting at the base of his penis.

When it stopped, Trinity and I peered at one another and grinned. It looked like we were going to have one last chance to reconnect in the workshop after all.

"It looks like we have our winners," Laila nodded,

leaning over to inspect the final position of the balls. "Would Trinity and Jade like to join us in the middle of the circle for our final demonstration?"

The two of us crawled teasingly toward the futon and when we sat down beside Alessandro, his dick twitched between his legs, slapping up against his stomach.

"I thought you only liked to fuck *chicks*?" I whispered to Trinity, sitting beside me.

"In this case I'm willing to make an exception," she smiled. "Especially if it means I get one more chance to fuck you also."

"Okay," Laila said, clearing the nerf balls off the surface of the futon. "In this last position I call the *International House of Pancakes*, the women are going to be stacked a little differently. In this case, Alessandro will have a *choice* as to where he chooses to place his tool. I'd like the two of you to lie down in the missionary position, with your knees pulled up as far as you can to facilitate Alessandro's freedom of access."

Trinity and I glanced at one another and smiled.

"Top or bottom?" I said.

She took one look at Alessandro's dripping pole and grinned.

"I think I'll take the bottom position this time."

She lay down on the futon and pulled her knees up onto her chest then I squatted overtop of her, placing the underside of my thighs overtop of hers, slowly lowering myself until my mound touched hers with our pussies gaping open like two yawning cats.

While Alessandro stared at our dripping kitties like a kid in a candy store, Laila peered at him, cocking her head.

"What are you waiting for?" she said. "It looks to me like you've got your choice of two eager beavers."

"Does it only have to be only *one*?" he grinned.

"What do you think, ladies?" Laila said. "Are you open to a little game of *hide the hot dog*?"

"Works for me," I nodded, grinding my mound excitedly against Trinity's.

"If you want to season your sausage with some extra juices," Trinity smiled. "Have at it."

Alessandro paused for a moment, peering at Laila with puppy dog eyes.

"Am I allowed to go all the way this time?" he said.

"If by all the way you mean *climaxing*, I'd say you've deserved that right after watching all the other girls come this afternoon."

Alessandro tilted his head to peer at Trinity and me kissing softly while we rolled our hips expectantly together.

"Do you want me to use a condom?" he said.

"*Hell*, no," I said. "That would just ruin it for me. I'm on the pill, so there's no need to worry on my part."

"And I'm not at that stage in my cycle, so there's no risk for me either," Trinity nodded.

"Alright then," Alessandro said, crawling up on his knees toward the junction of our pussies, slapping his hard pole against the side of my cheeks. "Let's get this party started."

While Trinity and I groaned into each other's mouths, he grasped his organ with two fingers and swiped it slowly up and down the length of our two slits, circling it teasingly over each of our clits.

"Ungh," I grunted, tilting my hips forward to press our clits together. "Place that hunk of bacon between our hotcakes," I said, echoing Laila's house of pancakes description. "There's plenty of syrup between the two of us to slide it in."

"Mmm," Alessandro hummed, deciding which of our dripping holes he wanted to fuck first.

When I felt him sliding his thick erection into my slit, I groaned, sliding my tits against Trinity's sweaty breasts.

"Fuck, yes," I grunted. "Plow me with that big dick. This is the sweetest dildo you've introduced so far, Laila."

"Glad you're enjoying it," she smiled, tilting her head down to peer at Trinity panting underneath me. "How about you, Trinity? Are you enjoying the experience just as much?"

"I can actually feel Alessandro's big prick thrusting into Jade's pussy while she rests on top of me," she nodded. "It's a feeling I've never experienced before..."

"Is it adding a new dimension to your tribbing experience?" she said, remembering how Trinity had introduced herself as a hardcore lesbian.

"Definitely," she grunted. "Alessandro's hips pressing against Jade's butt is sliding her clit overtop of mine while I feel his balls slapping against my pussy. I might need to invite some of my gay friends into my lovemaking routine after this."

"In that case," Laila said. "Would you like to feel his tool stimulating you more directly?"

"As long as Jade doesn't mind sharing the *bacon*," she smiled.

"Go for it, girl," I nodded. "I'm happy either way. Between the two of you, I'm getting stimulated in all the right places."

Alessandro pounded my ass for a few more strokes, then he pulled out of my hole and inserted his prick into Trinity's slit, driving his hips quickly forward.

"Aghh," Trinity grunted when she felt Alessandro's dick hit the back of her pussy.

"Are you sure you're okay with this, babe?" I said, tilting my head to look into her eyes.

"Are you kidding me?" she groaned, pulling my face back toward hers. "I've been waiting to feel a warm dick inside me all afternoon. Rub your clit against me while he fucks me with that big sausage."

"Mmm," I moaned into her mouth while Alessandro rocked our bodies back and forth over the heaving mattress.

I could feel the stubble on his mound scraping against the edge of my anus while he plowed Trinity's pussy, and I tilted my hips harder downward, pressing my clit over Trinity's mound.

"Oh fuck," Trinity gasped, feeling her vulva being stimulated from two directions. "Pound me with your big cock, Alessandro. I'm going to come soon..."

"Wait for me, baby," I moaned, rocking my hips harder against her sopping pussy and Alessandro's hard stomach. "Let's show this stud what a real fountain of Venus feels like."

As Alessandro began to rock his hips faster against our butts, he gripped the sides of my buttocks, sinking his fingers hard into my flesh. Realizing he was getting close to his limit, I angled my hips downward a few more inches, then I let rip with the most explosive orgasm in my three days of the workshop. When Trinity felt me squirting hard over her upturned pussy, she grunted loudly, shaking her tits against mine. When Alessandro felt her spraying her juices against the underside of his tightening balls, he also lost control, howling as he sunk his organ deep into her hole while she clamped her pussy against his pulsating tool.

As the three of us wailed in simultaneous ecstasy, I heard loud grunting coming from around the circle where the rest of the women were busy pounding each other with their strap-on dildos. Even Laila had joined in on the action, holding a buzzing We-Vibe vibrator against her quivering pussy while she pressed the two ends inside her dripping vulva. By the time all of us finished shaking and moaning, the entire room was filled with the erotic scent of sex emanating from every corner.

*Fuck me*, I smiled to myself while I lay panting atop Trinity's still-heaving stomach. *Who knew tribbing could have so many stimulating combinations and permutations?*

---

R eady for more erotic chills and thrills? Read the next exciting volume in Jade's Erotic Adventures:

*There's a reason the tongue has more muscles than any other body organ...*

# ALSO BY VICTORIA RUSH

*Wet your whistle a hundred different ways with Jade's Erotic Adventures. Browse the full collection of Victoria Rush steamy stories here:*

*Click to scan your favorites...*

# FOLLOW VICTORIA RUSH:

*Want to keep informed of my latest erotic book releases? Sign up for my newsletter and receive a FREE bonus book:*

*Spying on the neighbors just got a lot more interesting...*